Chimneysmoke

Christopher Morley

Chimneysmoke

ISBN: 978-1-64799-703-8

CONTENTS

iv

AUTHOR'S NOTE

There are a number of poems in this collection that have not previously appeared in book form. But, as a few readers may discern, many of the verses are reprinted from Songs for a Little House (1917), The Rocking Horse (1919) and Hide and Seek (1920). There is also one piece revived from the judicious obscurity of an early escapade, The Eighth Sin, published in Oxford in 1912. It is on Mr. Thomas Fogarty's delightful and sympathetic drawings that this book rests its real claim to be considered a new venture. To Mr. Fogarty, and to Mr. George H. Doran, whose constant kindness and generosity contradict all the traditions about publishers and minor poets, the author expresses his permanent gratitude.

Roslyn, Long Island

TO THE LITTLE HOUSE

Dear little house, dear shabby street,
Dear books and beds and food to eat!
How feeble words are to express
The facets of your tenderness.

How white the sun comes through the pane!
In tinkling music drips the rain!
How burning bright the furnace glows!
What paths to shovel when it snows!

O dearly loved Long Island trains!
O well remembered joys and pains....
How near the housetops Beauty leans
Along that little street in Queens!

Let these poor rhymes abide for proof
Joy dwells beneath a humble roof;
Heaven is not built of country seats
But little queer suburban streets!

March, 1917

1

A GRACE BEFORE WRITING

This is a sacrament, I think!
Holding the bottle toward the light,
As blue as lupin gleams the ink;
May Truth be with me as I write!

That small dark cistern may afford
Reunion with some vanished friend,—
And with this ink I have just poured
May none but honest words be penned!

DEDICATION FOR A FIREPLACE

This hearth was built for thy delight,
For thee the logs were sawn,
For thee the largest chair, at night,
Is to the chimney drawn.

For thee, dear lass, the match was lit
To yield the ruddy blaze—
May Jack Frost give us joy of it
For many, many days

TAKING TITLE

To make this house my very own
Could not be done by law alone.
Though covenant and deed convey
Absolute fee, as lawyers say,
There are domestic rites beside
By which this house is sanctified.

By kindled fire upon the hearth,
By planted pansies in the garth,
By food, and by the quiet rest
Of those brown eyes that I love best,
And by a friend's bright gift of wine,
I dedicate this house of mine.

When all but I are soft abed
I trail about my quiet stead
A wreath of blue tobacco smoke
(A charm that evil never broke)
And bring my ritual to an end
By giving shelter to a friend.

These done, O dwelling, you become
Not just a house, but truly Home!

THE SECRET

It was the House of Quietness
To which I came at dusk;
The garth was lit with roses
And heavy with their musk.

The tremulous tall poplar trees
Stood whispering around,
The gentle flicker of their plumes
More quiet than no sound.

And as I wondered at the door
What magic might be there,
The Lady of Sweet Silences
Came softly down the stair.

ONLY A MATTER OF TIME

Down-slipping Time, sweet, swift, and shallow stream,
Here, like a boulder, lies this afternoon
Across your eager flow. So you shall stay,
Deepened and dammed, to let me breathe and be.
Your troubled fluency, your running gleam
Shall pause, and circle idly, still and clear:
The while I lie and search your glassy pool
Where, gently coiling in their lazy round,
Unseparable minutes drift and swim,
Eddy and rise and brim. And I will see
How many crystal bubbles of slack Time
The mind can hold and cherish in one Now!

Now, for one conscious vacancy of sense,
The stream is gathered in a deepening pond,
Not a mere moving mirror. Through the sharp
Correct reflection of the standing scene
The mind can dip, and cleanse itself with rest,
And see, slow spinning in the lucid gold,
Your liquid motes, imperishable Time.

It cannot be. The runnel slips away:
The clear smooth downward sluice begins again,
More brightly slanting for that trembling pause,
Leaving the sense its conscious vague unease
As when a sonnet flashes on the mind,
Trembles and burns an instant, and is gone.

AT THE MERMAID CAFETERIA

Truth is enough for prose:
Calmly it goes
To tell just what it knows.

For verse, skill will suffice—
Delicate, nice
Casting of verbal dice.

Poetry, men attain
By subtler pain
More flagrant in the brain—

An honesty unfeigned,
A heart unchained,
A madness well restrained.

OUR HOUSE

It should be yours, if I could build
The quaint old dwelling I desire,
With books and pictures bravely filled
And chairs beside an open fire,
White-panelled rooms with candles lit—
I lie awake to think of it!

A dial for the sunny hours,
A garden of old-fashioned flowers—
Say marigolds and lavender
And mignonette and fever-few,
And Judas-tree and maidenhair
And candytuft and thyme and rue—
All these for you to wander in.

A Chinese carp (called Mandarin)
Waving a sluggish silver fin
Deep in the moat: so tame he comes
To lip your fingers offering crumbs.
Tall chimneys, like long listening ears,
White shutters, ivy green and thick,
And walls of ruddy Tudor brick
Grown mellow with the passing years.
And windows with small leaded panes,
Broad window-seats for when it rains;
A big blue bowl of pot pourri
And—yes, a Spanish chestnut tree
To coin the autumn's minted gold.

A summer house for drinking tea —
All these (just think!) for you and me.

A staircase of the old black wood
Cut in the days of Robin Hood,
And banisters worn smooth as glass
Down which your hand will lightly pass;
A piano with pale yellow keys
For wistful twilight melodies,
And dusty bottles in a bin —
All these for you to revel in!

But when? Ah well, until that time
We'll habit in this house of rhyme.

1912

ON NAMING A HOUSE

When I a householder became
I had to give my house a name.

I thought I'd call it "Poplar Trees,"
Or "Widdershins" or "Velvet Bees,"
Or "Just Beneath a Star."
I thought of "House Where Plumbings Freeze,"
Or "As You Like it," "If You Please,"
Or "Nicotine" or "Bread and Cheese,"
"Full Moon" or "Doors Ajar."

But still I sought some subtle charm,
Some rune to guard my roof from harm
And keep the devil far;
I thought of this, and I was saved!
I had my letter-heads engraved
         The House Where Brown Eyes Are.

A HALLOWE'EN MEMORY

Do you remember, Heart's Desire,
The night when Hallowe'en first came?
The newly dedicated fire,
The hearth unsanctified by flame?

How anxiously we swept the bricks
(How tragic, were the draught not right!)
And then the blaze enwrapped the sticks
And filled the room with dancing light.

We could not speak, but only gaze,
Nor half believe what we had seen—
Our home, our hearth, our golden blaze,
Our cider mugs, our Hallowe'en!

And then a thought occurred to me—
We ran outside with sudden shout
And looked up at the roof, to see
Our own dear smoke come drifting out.

And of all man's felicities
The very subtlest one, say I,
Is when, for the first time, he sees
His hearthfire smoke against the sky.

REFUSING YOU IMMORTALITY

If I should tell, unstinted,
Your beauty and your grace,
All future lads would whisper
Traditions of your face;
If I made public tumult
Your mirth, your queenly state,
Posterity would grumble
That it was born too late.

I will not frame your beauty
In bright undying phrase,
Nor blaze it as a legend
For unborn men to praise —
For why should future lovers
Be saddened and depressed?
Deluded, let them fancy
Their own girls loveliest!

BAYBERRY CANDLES

Dear sweet, when dusk comes up the hill,
The fire leaps high with golden prongs;
I place along the chimneysill
The tiny candles of my songs.
And though unsteadily they burn,
As evening shades from gray to blue
Like candles they will surely learn
To shine more clear, for love of you.

SECRET LAUGHTER

"I had a secret laughter."
—*Walter de la Mare.*

There is a secret laughter
That often comes to me,
And though I go about my work
As humble as can be,
There is no prince or prelate
I envy—no, not one.
No evil can befall me—
By God, I have a son!

SIX WEEKS OLD

He is so small, he does not know
The summer sun, the winter snow;
The spring that ebbs and comes again,
All this is far beyond his ken.

A little world he feels and sees:
His mother's arms, his mother's knees;
He hides his face against her breast,
And does not care to learn the rest.

A CHARM

For Our New Fireplace,
To Stop Its Smoking

O wood, burn bright; O flame, be quick;
O smoke, draw cleanly up the flue—
My lady chose your every brick
And sets her dearest hopes on you!

Logs cannot burn, nor tea be sweet,
Nor white bread turn to crispy toast,
Until the charm be made complete
By love, to lay the sooty ghost.

And then, dear books, dear waiting chairs,
Dear china and mahogany,
Draw close, for on the happy stairs
My brown-eyed girl comes down for tea!

MY PIPE

My pipe is old
And caked with soot;
My wife remarks:
"How can you put
That horrid relic,
So unclean,
Inside your mouth?
The nicotine
Is strong enough
To stupefy
A Swedish plumber."
I reply:

"This is the kind
Of pipe I like:
I fill it full
Of Happy Strike,
Or Barking Cat
Or Cabman's Puff,
Or Brooklyn Bridge
(That potent stuff)
Or Chaste Embraces,
Knacker's Twist,
Old Honeycomb
Or Niggerfist.

I clamp my teeth
Upon its stem—

It is my bliss,
My diadem.
Whatever Fate
May do to me,
This is my favorite
B
B B.
For this dear pipe
You feign to scorn
I smoked the night
The boy was born."

THE 5:42

Lilac, violet, and rose
Ardently the city glows;
Sunset glory, purely sweet,
Gilds the dreaming byway-street,
And, above the Avenue,
Winter dusk is deepening blue.

(Then, across Long Island meadows,
Darker, darker, grow the shadows:
Patience, little waiting lass!
Laggard minutes slowly pass;
Patience, laughs the yellow fire:
Homeward bound is heart's desire!)

Hark, adown the canyon street
Flows the merry tide of feet;
High the golden buildings loom
Blazing in the purple gloom;
All the town is set with stars,
Homeward chant the Broadway cars!

All down Thirty-second Street
Homeward, Homeward, say the feet!
Tramping men, uncouth to view,
Footsore, weary, thrill anew;
Gone the ringing telephones,
Blessed nightfall now atones,

Casting brightness on the snow
Golden the train windows go.

Then (how long it seems) at last
All the way is overpast.
Heart that beats your muffled drum,
Lo, your venturer is come!
Wide the door! Leap high, O fire!
Home at length is heart's desire!
Gone is weariness and fret,
At the sill warm lips are met.
Once again may be renewed
The conjoined beatitude.

PETER PAN

*"The boy for whom Barrie wrote Peter Pan—the original of Peter Pan—
has died in battle."*

—*New York Times.*

And Peter Pan is dead? Not so!
When mothers turn the lights down low
And tuck their little sons in bed,
They know that Peter is not dead....

That little rounded blanket-hill;
Those prayer-time eyes, so deep and still—
However wise and great a man
He grows, he still is Peter Pan.

And mothers' ways are often queer:
They pause in doorways, just to hear
A tiny breathing; think a prayer;
And then go tiptoe down the stair.

IN HONOR OF TAFFY TOPAZ

Taffy, the topaz-colored cat,
Thinks now of this and now of that,
But chiefly of his meals.
Asparagus, and cream, and fish,
Are objects of his Freudian wish;
What you don't give, he steals.

His gallant heart is strongly stirred
By clink of plate or flight of bird,
He has a plumy tail;
At night he treads on stealthy pad
As merry as Sir Galahad
A-seeking of the Grail.

His amiable amber eyes
Are very friendly, very wise;
Like Buddha, grave and fat,
He sits, regardless of applause,
And thinking, as he kneads his paws,
What fun to be a cat!

THE CEDAR CHEST

Her mind is like her cedar chest
Wherein in quietness do rest
The wistful dreamings of her heart
In fragrant folds all laid apart.

There, put away in sprigs of rhyme
Until her life's full blossom-time,
Flutter (like tremulous little birds)
Her small and sweet maternal words.

READING ALOUD

Once we read Tennyson aloud
In our great fireside chair;
Between the lines, my lips could touch
Her April-scented hair.

How very fond I was, to think
The printed poems fair,
When close within my arms I held
A living lyric there!

ANIMAL CRACKERS

Animal crackers, and cocoa to drink,
That is the finest of suppers, I think;
When I'm grown up and can have what I please
I think I shall always insist upon these.

What do you choose when you're offered a treat?
When Mother says, "What would you like best to eat?"
Is it waffles and syrup, or cinnamon toast?
It's cocoa and animals that I love most!

The kitchen's the cosiest place that I know:
The kettle is singing, the stove is aglow,
And there in the twilight, how jolly to see
The cocoa and animals waiting for me.

Daddy and Mother dine later in state,
With Mary to cook for them, Susan to wait;
But they don't have nearly as much fun as I
Who eat in the kitchen with Nurse standing by;
And Daddy once said, he would like to be me
Having cocoa and animals once more for tea!

THE MILKMAN

Early in the morning, when the dawn is on the roofs,
You hear his wheels come rolling, you hear his horse's hoofs;
You hear the bottles clinking, and then he drives away:
You yawn in bed, turn over, and begin another day!

The old-time dairy maids are dear to every poet's heart—
I'd rather be the dairy man and drive a little cart,
And bustle round the village in the early morning blue,
And hang my reins upon a hook, as I've seen Casey do.

LIGHT VERSE

At night the gas lamps light our street,
Electric bulbs our homes;
The gas is billed in cubic feet,
Electric light in ohms.

But one illumination still
Is brighter far, and sweeter;
It is not figured in a bill,
Nor measured by a meter.

More bright than lights that money buys,
More pleasing to discerners,
The shining lamps of Helen's eyes,
Those lovely double burners!

THE FURNACE

At night I opened
The furnace door:
The warm glow brightened
The cellar floor.

The fire that sparkled
Blue and red,
Kept small toes cosy
In their bed.

As up the stair
So late I stole,
I said my prayer:
Thank God for coal!

WASHING THE DISHES

When we on simple rations sup
How easy is the washing up!
But heavy feeding complicates
The task by soiling many plates.

And though I grant that I have prayed
That we might find a serving-maid,
I'd scullion all my days, I think,
To see Her smile across the sink!

I wash, She wipes. In water hot
I souse each dish and pan and pot;
While Taffy mutters, purrs, and begs,
And rubs himself against my legs.

The man who never in his life
Has washed the dishes with his wife
Or polished up the silver plate—
He still is largely celibate.

One warning: there is certain ware
That must be handled with all care:
The Lord Himself will give you up
If you should drop a willow cup!

THE CHURCH OF UNBENT KNEES

As I went by the church to-day
I heard the organ cry;
And goodly folk were on their knees,
But I went striding by.

My minster hath a roof more vast:
My aisles are oak trees high;
My altar-cloth is on the hills,
My organ is the sky.

I see my rood upon the clouds,
The winds, my chanted choir;
My crystal windows, heaven-glazed,
Are stained with sunset fire.

The stars, the thunder, and the rain,
White sands and purple seas—
These are His pulpit and His pew,
My God of Unbent Knees!

ELEGY WRITTEN IN A COUNTRY COAL-BIN

The furnace tolls the knell of falling steam,
The coal supply is virtually done,
And at this price, indeed it does not seem
As though we could afford another ton.

Now fades the glossy, cherished anthracite;
The radiators lose their temperature:
How ill avail, on such a frosty night,
The "short and simple flannels of the poor."

Though in the icebox, fresh and newly laid,
The rude forefathers of the omelet sleep,
No eggs for breakfast till the bill is paid:
We cannot cook again till coal is cheap.

Can Morris-chair or papier-mâché bust
Revivify the failing pressure-gauge?
Chop up the grand piano if you must,
And burn the East Aurora parrot-cage!

Full many a can of purest kerosene
The dark unfathomed tanks of Standard Oil
Shall furnish me, and with their aid I mean
To bring my morning coffee to a boil.

THE OLD SWIMMER

I often wander on the beach
Where once, so brown of limb,
The biting air, the roaring surf
Summoned me to swim.

I see my old abundant youth
Where combers lean and spill,
And though I taste the foam no more
Other swimmers will.

Oh, good exultant strength to meet
The arching wall of green,
To break the crystal, swirl, emerge
Dripping, taut, and clean.

To climb the moving hilly blue,
To dive in ecstasy
And feel the salty chill embrace
Arm and rib and knee.

What brave and vanished laughter then
And tingling thighs to run,
 What warm and comfortable sands
Dreaming in the sun.
The crumbling water spreads in snow,
The surf is hissing still,
And though I kiss the salt no more
Other swimmers will.

32

THE MOON-SHEEP

The moon seems like a docile sheep,
She pastures while all people sleep;
But sometimes, when she goes astray,
She wanders all alone by day.

Up in the clear blue morning air
We are surprised to see her there,
Grazing in her woolly white,
Waiting the return of night.

When dusk lets down the meadow bars
She greets again her lambs, the stars!

SMELLS

Why is it that the poets tell
So little of the sense of smell?
These are the odors I love well:

The smell of coffee freshly ground;
Or rich plum pudding, holly crowned;
Or onions fried and deeply browned.

The fragrance of a fumy pipe;
The smell of apples, newly ripe;
And printers' ink on leaden type.

Woods by moonlight in September
Breathe most sweet; and I remember
Many a smoky camp-fire ember.

Camphor, turpentine, and tea,
The balsam of a Christmas tree,
These are whiffs of gramarye ...
A ship smells best of all to me!

SMELLS (JUNIOR)

My Daddy smells like tobacco and books,
Mother, like lavender and listerine;
Uncle John carries a whiff of cigars,
Nannie smells starchy and soapy and clean.

Shandy, my dog, has a smell of his own
(When he's been out in the rain he smells most);
But Katie, the cook, is more splendid than all—
She smells exactly like hot buttered toast!

MAR QUONG, CHINESE LAUNDRYMAN

I like the Chinese laundryman:
He smokes a pipe that bubbles,
And seems, as far as I can tell,
A man with but few troubles.
He has much to do, no doubt,
But also much to think about.

Most men (for instance I myself)
Are spending, at all times,
All our hard-earned quarters,
Our nickels and our dimes:
With Mar Quong it's the other way—
He takes in small change every day.

Next time you call for collars
In his steamy little shop,
Observe how tight his pigtail
Is coiled and piled on top.
But late at night he lets it hang
And thinks of the Yang-tse-kiang.

THE FAT LITTLE PURSE

On Saturdays, after the baby
Is bathed, fed, and sleeping serene,
His mother, as quickly as may be,
Arranges the household routine.
She rapidly makes herself pretty
And leaves the young limb with his nurse,
Then gaily she starts for the city,
And with her the fat little purse.

She trips through the crowd at the station,
To the rendezvous spot where we meet,
And keeping her eyes from temptation,
She avoids the most windowy street!
She is off for the Weekly Adventure;
To her comrade for better and worse
She says, "Never mind, when you've spent your
Last bit, here's the fat little purse."

Apart, in her thrifty exchequer,
She has hidden what must not be spent:
Enough for the butcher and baker,
Katie's wages, and milkman, and rent;
But the rest of her brave little treasure
She is gleeful and prompt to disburse—
What a richness of innocent pleasure
Can come from her fat little purse!

But either by giving or buying,

The little purse does not stay fat—
Perhaps it's a ragged child crying,
Perhaps it's a "pert little hat."
And the bonny brown eyes that were brightened
By pleasures so quaint and diverse,
Look up at me, wistful and frightened,
To see such a thin little purse.

The wisest of all financiering
Is that which is done by our wives:
By some little known profiteering
They add twos and twos and make fives;
And, husband, if you would be learning
The secret of thrift, it is terse:
Invest the great part of your earning
In her little, fat little purse.

THE REFLECTION
(To N. B. D.)

I have not heard her voice, nor seen her face,
Nor touched her hand;
And yet some echo of her woman's grace
I understand.

I have no picture of her lovelihood,
Her smile, her tint;
But that she is both beautiful and good
I have true hint.

In all that my friend thinks and says, I see
Her mirror true;
His thought of her is gentle; she must be
All gentle too.

In all his grief or laughter, work or play,
Each mood and whim,
How brave and tender, day by common day,
She speaks through him!

Therefore I say I know her, be her face>
Or dark or fair—
For when he shows his heart's most secret place
I see her there!

THE BALLOON PEDDLER

Who is the man on Chestnut street
With colored toy balloons?
I see him with his airy freight
On sunny afternoons—
A peddler of such lovely goods!
The heart leaps to behold
His mass of bubbles, red and green
And blue and pink and gold.

For sure that noble peddler man
Hath antic merchandise:
His toys that float and swim in air
Attract my eager eyes.
Perhaps he is a changeling prince
Bewitched through magic moons
To tempt us solemn busy folk
With meaningless balloons.

Beware, oh, valiant merchantman,
Tread cautious on the pave!
Lest some day come some realist,
Some haggard soul and grave,
A puritan efficientist
Who deems thy toys a sin—
He'll stalk thee madly from behind
And prick them with a pin!

LINES FOR AN ECCENTRIC'S BOOK PLATE

To use my books all friends are bid:
My shelves are open for 'em;
And in each one, as Grolier did,
I write Et Amicorum.

All lovely things in truth belong
To him who best employs them;
The house, the picture and the song
Are his who most enjoys them.

Perhaps this book holds precious lore,
And you may best discern it.
If you appreciate it more
Than I—why don't return it!

TO A POST-OFFICE INKWELL

How many humble hearts have dipped
In you, and scrawled their manuscript!
Have shared their secrets, told their cares,
Their curious and quaint affairs!

Your pool of ink, your scratchy pen,
Have moved the lives of unborn men,
And watched young people, breathing hard,
Put Heaven on a postal card.

THE CRIB

I sought immortality
Here and there—
I sent my rockets
Into the air:
I gave my name
A hostage to ink;
I dined a critic
And bought him drink.

I spurned the weariness
Of the flesh;
Denied fatigue
And began afresh—
If men knew all,
How they would laugh!
I even planned
My epitaph....

And then one night
When the dusk was thin
I heard the nursery
Rites begin:

I heard the tender
Soothings said
Over a crib, and
A small sweet head.

Then in a flash
It came to me
That there was my
Immortality!

THE POET

The barren music of a word or phrase,
The futile arts of syllable and stress,
He sought. The poetry of common days
He did not guess.

The simplest, sweetest rhythms life affords—
Unselfish love, true effort truly done,
The tender themes that underlie all words—
He knew not one.

The human cadence and the subtle chime
Of little laughters, home and child and wife,
He knew not. Artist merely in his rhyme,
Not in his life.

TO A DISCARDED MIRROR

DEAR glass, before your silver pane
My lady used to tend her hair;
And yet I search your disc in vain
To find some shadow of her there.

I thought your magic, deep and bright,
Might still some dear reflection hold:
Some glint of eyes or shoulders white,
Some flash of gowns she wore of old.

Your polished round must still recall
The laughing face, the neck like snow—
Remember, on your lonely wall,
That Helen used you long ago!

[TN: Mirror Image Translated below.]

Dear glass, before your silver pane
My lady used to tend her hair;
And yet I search your disc in vain
To find some shadow of her there.

I thought your magic, deep and bright,
Might still some dear reflection hold:
Some glint of eyes or shoulders white,
Some flash of gowns she wore of old.

Your polished round must still recall
The laughing face, the neck like snow—
Remember, on your lonely wall,
That Helen used you long ago!

TO A CHILD

The greatest poem ever known
Is one all poets have outgrown:
The poetry, innate, untold,
Of being only four years old.

Still young enough to be a part
Of Nature's great impulsive heart,
Born comrade of bird, beast and tree
And unselfconscious as the bee —

And yet with lovely reason skilled
Each day new paradise to build;
Elate explorer of each sense,
Without dismay, without pretence!

In your unstained transparent eyes
There is no conscience, no surprise:
Life's queer conundrums you accept,
Your strange divinity still kept.

 Being, that now absorbs you, all
Harmonious, unit, integral,
Will shred into perplexing bits, —
Oh, contradictions of the wits!

And Life, that sets all things in rhyme,
May make you poet, too, in time —
But there were days, O tender elf,
When you were Poetry itself!

TO A VERY YOUNG GENTLEMAN

My child, what painful vistas are before you!
What years of youthful ills and pangs and bumps—
Indignities from aunts who "just adore" you,
And chicken-pox and measles, croup and mumps!
I don't wish to dismay you,—it's not fair to,
Promoted now from bassinet to crib,—
But, O my babe, what troubles flesh is heir to
Since God first made so free with Adam's rib!

Laboriously you will proceed with teething;
When teeth are here, you'll meet the dentist's chair;
They'll teach you ways of walking, eating, breathing,
That stoves are hot, and how to brush your hair;
And so, my poor, undaunted little stripling,
By bruises, tears, and trousers you will grow,
And, borrowing a leaf from Mr. Kipling,
I'll wish you luck, and moralize you so:

If you can think up seven thousand methods
Of giving cooks and parents heart disease;
Can rifle pantry-shelves, and then give death odds
By water, fire, and falling out of trees;
If you can fill your every boyish minute
With sixty seconds' worth of mischief done,
Yours is the house and everything that's in it,
And, which is more, you'll be your father's son!

TO AN OLD-FASHIONED POET

(Lizette Woodworth Reese)
Most tender poet, when the gods confer
They save your gracile songs a nook apart,
And bless with Time's untainted lavender
The ageless April of your singing heart.

You, in an age unbridled, ne'er declined
The appointed patience that the Muse decrees,
Until, deep in the flower of the mind
The hovering words alight, like bridegroom bees.

By casual praise or casual blame unstirred
The placid gods grant gifts where they belong:
To you, who understand, the perfect word,
The recompensed necessities of song.

BURNING LEAVES IN SPRING

When withered leaves are lost in flame
Their eddying ghosts, a thin blue haze,
Blow through the thickets whence they came
On amberlucent autumn days.

The cool green woodland heart receives
Their dim, dissolving, phantom breath;
In young hereditary leaves
They see their happy life-in-death.

My minutes perish as they glow —
Time burns my crazy bonfire through;
But ghosts of blackened hours still blow,
Eternal Beauty, back to you!

BURNING LEAVES, NOVEMBER

These are folios of April,
All the library of spring,
Missals gilt and rubricated
With the frost's illumining.

Ruthless, we destroy these treasures,
Set the torch with hand profane—
Gone, like Alexandrian vellums,
Like the books of burnt Louvain!
Yet these classics are immortal:
O collectors, have no fear,
For the publisher will issue
New editions every year.

A VALENTINE GAME

(For Two Players)

They have a game, thus played:
He says unto his maid
What are those shining things
So brown, so golden brown?
And she, in doubt, replies
How now, what shining things
So brown?

But then, she coming near,
To see more clear,
He looks again, and cries
(All startled with surprise)
Sweet wretch, they are your eyes,
So brown, so brown!

The climax and the end consist
In kissing, and in being kissed.

FOR A BIRTHDAY

At two years old the world he sees
Must seem expressly made to please!
Such new-found words and games to try,
Such sudden mirth, he knows not why,
So many curiosities!

As life about him, by degrees
Discloses all its pageantries
He watches with approval shy
At two years old.

With wonders tired he takes his ease
At dusk, upon his mother's knees:
A little laugh, a little cry,
Put toys to bed, then "seepy-bye"—
The world is made of such as these
At two years old.

KEATS

(1821-1921)

When sometimes, on a moony night, I've passed
A street-lamp, seen my doubled shadow flee,
I've noticed how much darker, clearer cast,
The full moon poured her silhouette of me.

Just so of spirits. Beauty's silver light
Limns with a ray more pure, and tenderer too:
Men's clumsy gestures, to unearthly sight,
Surpass the shapes they show by human view.

On this brave world, where few such meteors fell,
Her youngest son, to save us, Beauty flung.
He suffered and descended into hell—
And comforts yet the ardent and the young.

Drunken of moonlight, dazed by draughts of sky,
Dizzy with stars, his mortal fever ran:
His utterance a moon-enchanted cry
Not free from folly—for he too was man.

And now and here, a hundred years away,
Where topless towers shadow golden streets,
The young men sit, nooked in a cheap café,
Perfectly happy ... talking about Keats.

TO H. F. M.

A SONNET IN SUNLIGHT

This is a day for sonnets: Oh how clear
Our splendid cliffs and summits lift the gaze—
If all the perfect moments of the year
Were poured and gathered in one sudden blaze,
Then, then perhaps, in some endowered phrase
My flat strewn words would rise and come more near
To tell of you. Your beauty and your praise
Would fall like sunlight on this paper here.

Then I would build a sonnet that would stand
Proud and perennial on this pale bright sky;
So tall, so steep, that it might stay the hand
Of Time, the dusty wrecker. He would sigh
To tear my strong words down. And he would say:
"That song he built for her, one summer day."

QUICKENING

Such little, puny things are words in rhyme:
Poor feeble loops and strokes as frail as hairs;
You see them printed here, and mark their chime,
And turn to your more durable affairs.
Yet on such petty tools the poet dares
To run his race with mortar, bricks and lime,
And draws his frail stick to the point, and stares
To aim his arrow at the heart of Time.

Intangible, yet pressing, hemming in,
This measured emptiness engulfs us all,
And yet he points his paper javelin
And sees it eddy, waver, turn, and fall,
And feels, between delight and trouble torn,
The stirring of a sonnet still unborn.

AT A WINDOW SILL

To write a sonnet needs a quiet mind....
I paused and pondered, tried again. To write....
Raising the sash, I breathed the winter night:
Papers and small hot room were left behind.
Against the gusty purple, ribbed and spined
With golden slots and vertebræ of light
Men's cages loomed. Down sliding from a height
An elevator winked as it declined.

Coward! There is no quiet in the brain—
If pity burns it not, then beauty will:
Tinder it is for every blowing spark.
Uncertain whether this is bliss or pain
The unresting mind will gaze across the sill
From high apartment windows, in the dark.

THE RIVER OF LIGHT

I. Broadway, 103rd to 96th.

Lights foam and bubble down the gentle grade:
Bright shine chop sueys and rôtisseries;
In pink translucence glowingly displayed
See camisole and stocking and chemise.
Delicatessen windows full of cheese—
Above, the chimes of church-bells toll and fade—
And then, from off some distant Palisade
That gluey savor on the Jersey breeze!

The burning bulbs, in green and white and red,
Spell out a Change of Program Sun., Wed., Fri.,
A clicking taxi spins with ruby spark.
There is a sense of poising near the head
Of some great flume of brightness, flowing by
To pour in gathering torrent through the dark.

II. Below 96th

The current quickens, and in golden flow
Hurries its flotsam downward through the night—
Here are the rapids where the undertow
Whirls endless motors in a gleaming flight.
From blazing tributaries, left and right,
Influent streams of blue and amber grow.
Columbus Circle eddies: all below
Is pouring flame, a gorge of broken light.

See how the burning river boils in spate,
Channeled by cliffs of insane jewelry,
Painting a rosy roof on cloudy air—
And just about ten minutes after eight,
Tossing a surf of color to the sky
It bursts in cataracts upon Times Square!

OF HER GLORIOUS MADNESS

The city's mad: through her prodigious veins
What errant, strange, eccentric humors thrill:
Day, when her cataracts of sunlight spill—
Night, golden-panelled with her window panes;
The toss of wind-blown skirts; and who can drill
Forever his fierce heart with checking reins?
Cruel and mad, my statisticians say—
Ah, but she raves in such a gallant way!

Brave madness, built for beauty and the sun—
In such a town who can be sane? Not I.
Of clashing colors all her moods are spun—
A scarlet anger and a golden cry.
This frantic town where madcap mischiefs run
They ask to take the veil, and be a nun!

IN AN AUCTION ROOM

(Letter of John Keats to Fanny Browne, Anderson Galleries, March 15, 1920.)

To Dr. A. S. W. Rosenbach.

H ow about this lot? said the auctioneer;
One hundred, may I say, just for a start?
Between the plum-red curtains, drawn apart,
A written sheet was held.... And strange to hear
(Dealer, would I were steadfast as thou art)
The cold quick bids. (Against you in the rear!)
The crimson salon, in a glow more clear
Burned bloodlike purple as the poet's heart.

Song that outgrew the singer! Bitter Love
That broke the proud hot heart it held in thrall;
Poor script, where still those tragic passions move —
Eight hundred bid: fair warning: the last call:
The soul of Adonais, like a star....
Sold for eight hundred dollars — Doctor R.!

EPITAPH FOR A POET WHO WROTE NO POETRY

"It is said that a poet has died young in the breast of the
   most stolid."—Robert Louis Stevenson.

What was the service of this poet? He Who blinked the
blinding dazzle-rays that run
Where life profiles its edges to the sun,
And still suspected much he could not see.
Clay-stopped, yet in his taciturnity
There lay the vein of glory, known to none;
And moods of secret smiling, only won
When peace and passion, time and sense, agree.

Fighting the world he loved for chance to brood,
Ignorant when to embrace, when to avoid
His loves that held him in their vital clutch—
This was his service, his beatitude;
This was the inward trouble he enjoyed
Who knew so little, and who felt so much.

SONNET BY A GEOMETER

THE CIRCLE

Few things are perfect: we bear Eden's scar;
Yet faulty man was godlike in design
That day when first, with stick and length of twine,
He drew me on the sand. Then what could mar
His joy in that obedient mystic line;
And then, computing with a zeal divine,
He called π 3-point-14159
And knew my lovely circuit 2 π r!

A circle is a happy thing to be—
Think how the joyful perpendicular
Erected at the kiss of tangency
Must meet my central point, my avatar!
They talk of 14 points: yet only 3
Determine every circle: **Q. E. D.**

TO A VAUDEVILLE TERRIER SEEN ON A LEASH, IN THE PARK

Three times a day—at two, at seven, at nine—
O terrier, you play your little part:
Absurd in coat and skirt you push a cart,
With inner anguish walk a tight-rope line.
Up there, before the hot and dazzling shine
You must be rigid servant of your art,
Nor watch those fluffy cats—your doggish heart
Might leap and then betray you with a whine!

But sometimes, when you've faithfully rehearsed,
Your trainer takes you walking in the park,
Straining to sniff the grass, to chase a frog.
The leash is slipped, and then your joy will burst—
Adorable it is to run and bark,
To be—alas, how seldom—just a dog!

TO AN OLD FRIEND

(For Lloyd Williams)

I like to dream of some established spot
Where you and I, old friend, an evening through
Under tobacco's fog, streaked gray and blue,
Might reconsider laughters unforgot.
Beside a hearth-glow, golden-clear and hot,
I'd hear you tell the oddities men do.
The clock would tick, and we would sit, we two—
Life holds such meetings for us, does it not?

Happy are men when they have learned to prize
The sure unvarnished virtue of their friends,
The unchanged kindness of a well-known face:
On old fidelities our world depends,
And runs a simple course in honest wise,
Not a mere taxicab shot wild through space!

TO A BURLESQUE SOUBRETTE

Upstage the great high-shafted beefy choir
Squawked in 2000 watts of orange glare—
You came, and impudent and deuce-may-care
Danced where the gutter flamed with footlight fire.

Flung from the roof, spots red and yellow burned
And followed you. The blatant brassy clang
Of instruments drowned out the words you sang,
But goldenly you capered, twirled and turned.

Boyish and slender, child-limbed, quick and proud,
A sprite of irresistible disdain,
Fair as a jonquil in an April rain,
You seemed too sweet an imp for that dull crowd....

And then, behind the scenes, I heard you say,
"O Gawd, I got a hellish cold to-day!"

THOUGHTS WHILE PACKING A TRUNK

The sonnet is a trunk, and you must pack
With care, to ship frail baggage far away;
The octet is the trunk; sestet, the tray;
Tight, but not overloaded, is the knack.
First, at the bottom, heavy thoughts you stack,
And in the chinks your adjectives you lay —
Your phrases, folded neatly as you may,
Stowing a syllable in every crack.

Then, in the tray, your daintier stuff is hid:
The tender quatrain where your moral sings —
Be careful, though, lest as you close the lid
You crush and crumple all these fragile things.
Your couplet snaps the hasps and turns the key —
Ship to The Editor, marked **C. O. D.**

STREETS

I have seen streets where strange enchantment broods:
Old ruddy houses where the morning shone
In seemly quiet on their tranquil moods,
Across the sills white curtains outward blown.
Their marble steps were scoured as white as bone
Where scrubbing housemaids toiled on wounded knee—
And yet, among all streets that I have known
These placid byways give least peace to me.

In such a house, where green light shining through
(From some back garden) framed her silhouette
I saw a girl, heard music blithely sung.
She stood there laughing, in a dress of blue,
And as I went on, slowly, there I met
An old, old woman, who had once been young.

TO THE ONLY BEGETTER

I

I have no hope to make you live in rhyme
Or with your beauty to enrich the years—
Enough for me this now, this present time;
The greater claim for greater sonneteers.
But O how covetous I am of NOW—
Dear human minutes, marred by human pains—
I want to know your lips, your cheek, your brow,
And all the miracles your heart contains,
I wish to study all your changing face,
Your eyes, divinely hurt with tenderness;
I hope to win your dear unstinted grace
For these blunt rhymes and what they would express.
Then may you say, when others better prove:—
"Theirs for their style I'll read, his for his love."

II

When all my trivial rhymes are blotted out,
Vanished our days, so precious and so few,
If some should wonder what we were about
And what the little happenings we knew:
I wish that they might know how, night by night,
My pencil, heavy in the sleepy hours,
Sought vainly for some gracious way to write

How much this love is ours, and only ours.
How many evenings, as you drowsed to sleep,
I read to you by tawny candle-glow,
And watched you down the valley dim and deep
Where poppies and the April flowers grow.
Then knelt beside your pillow with a prayer,
And loved the breath of pansies in your hair.

PEDOMETER

My thoughts beat out in sonnets while I walk,
And every evening on the homeward street
I find the rhythm of my marching feet
Throbs into verses (though the rhyme may balk).
I think the sonneteers were walking men:
The form is dour and rigid, like a clamp,
But with the swing of legs the tramp, tramp, tramp
Of syllables begins to thud, and then—
Lo! while you seek a rhyme for hook or crook
shed your shabby coat, and you are kith
To all great walk-and-singers—Meredith,
And Shakespeare, Wordsworth, Keats, and Rupert Brooke!
Free verse is poor for walking, but a sonnet—
O marvellous to stride and brood upon it!

HOSTAGES

"He that hath wife and children hath given hostages to fortune." —Bacon.

Aye, Fortune, thou hast hostage of my best!
I, that was once so heedless of thy frown,
Have armed thee cap-à-pie to strike me down,
Have given thee blades to hold against my breast.
My virtue, that was once all self-possessed,
Is parceled out in little hands, and brown
Bright eyes, and in a sleeping baby's gown:
To threaten these will put me to the test.

Sure, since there are these pitiful poor chinks
Upon the makeshift armor of my heart,
For thee no honor lies in such a fight!
And thou wouldst shame to vanquish one, me-thinks,
Who came awake with such a painful start
To hear the coughing of a child at night.

ARS DURA

How many evenings, walking soberly
Along our street all dappled with rich sun,
I please myself with words, and happily
Time rhymes to footfalls, planning how they run;
And yet, when midnight comes, and paper lies
Clean, white, receptive, all that one can ask,
Alas for drowsy spirit, weary eyes
And traitor hand that fails the well loved task!

Who ever learned the sonnet's bitter craft
But he had put away his sleep, his ease,
The wine he loved, the men with whom he laughed
To brood upon such thankless tricks as these?
And yet, such joy does in that craft abide
He greets the paper as the groom the bride!

O. HENRY—APOTHECARY

("O. Henry" once worked in a drug-store in Greensboro, N. C.)

Where once he measured camphor, glycerine,
Quinine and potash, peppermint in bars,
And all the oils and essences so keen
That druggists keep in rows of stoppered jars—
Now, blender of strange drugs more volatile,
The master pharmacist of joy and pain
Dispenses sadness tinctured with a smile
And laughter that dissolves in tears again.

O brave apothecary! You who knew
What dark and acid doses life prefers
And yet with friendly face resolved to brew
These sparkling potions for your customers—
In each prescription your Physician writ
You poured your rich compassion and your wit!

FOR THE CENTENARY OF KEATS'S SONNET

(1816)
"On First Looking Into Chapman's Homer."

I knew a scientist, an engineer,
Student of tensile strengths and calculus,
A man who loved a cantilever truss
And always wore a pencil on his ear.
My friend believed that poets all were queer,
And literary folk ridiculous;
But one night, when it chanced that three of us
Were reading Keats aloud, he stopped to hear.

Lo, a new planet swam into his ken!
His eager mind reached for it and took hold.
Ten years are by: I see him now and then,
And at alumni dinners, if cajoled,
He mumbles gravely, to the cheering men:—
Much have I travelled in the realms of gold.

TWO O'CLOCK

Night after night goes by: and clocks still chime
And stars are changing patterns in the dark,
And watches tick, and over-puissant Time
Benumbs the eager brain. The dogs that bark,
The trains that roar and rattle in the night,
The very cats that prowl, all quiet find
And leave the darkness empty, silent quite:
Sleep comes to chloroform the fretting mind.

So all things end: and what is left at last?
Some scribbled sonnets tossed upon the floor,
A memory of easy days gone past,
A run-down watch, a pipe, some clothes we wore—
And in the darkened room I lean to know
How warm her dreamless breath does pause and flow.

THE COMMERCIAL TRAVELLER

Ah very sweet! If news should come to you
Some afternoon, while waiting for our eve,
That the great Manager had made me leave
To travel on some territory new;
And that, whatever homeward winds there blew,
I could not touch your hand again, nor heave
The logs upon our hearth and bid you weave
Some wistful tale before the flames that grew....

Then, when the sudden tears had ceased to blind
Your pansied eyes, I wonder if you could
Remember rightly, and forget aright?
Remember just your lad, uncouthly good,
Forgetting when he failed in spleen or spite?
Could you remember him as always kind?

THE WEDDED LOVER

I read in our old journals of the days
When our first love was April-sweet and new,
How fair it blossomed and deep-rooted grew
Despite the adverse time; and our amaze
At moon and stars and beauty beyond praise
That burgeoned all about us: gold and blue
The heaven arched us in, and all we knew
Was gentleness. We walked on happy ways.

They said by now the path would be more steep,
The sunsets paler and less mild the air;
Rightly we heeded not: it was not true.
We will not tell the secret—let it keep.
I know not how I thought those days so fair
These being so much fairer, spent with you.

TO YOU, REMEMBERING THE PAST

When we were parted, sweet, and darkness came,
I used to strike a match, and hold the flame
Before your picture and would breathless mark
The answering glimmer of the tiny spark
That brought to life the magic of your eyes,
Their wistful tenderness, their glad surprise.

Holding that mimic torch before your shrine
I used to light your eyes and make them mine;
Watch them like stars set in a lonely sky,
Whisper my heart out, yearning for reply;
Summon your lips from far across the sea
Bidding them live a twilight hour with me.

Then, when the match was shrivelled into gloom,
Lo—you were with me in the darkened room.

CHARLES AND MARY

(December 27, 1834)

Lamb died just before I left town, and Mr. Ryle of the E. India House, one of his extors., notified it to me.... He said Miss L. was resigned and composed at the event, but it was from her malady, then in mild type, so that when she saw her brother dead, she observed on his beauty when asleep and apprehended nothing further.
—Letter of John Rickman, 24 January, 1835.

I hear their voices still: the stammering one
Struggling with some absurdity of jest;
Her quiet words that puzzle and protest
Against the latest outrage of his fun.
So wise, so simple—has she never guessed
That through his laughter, love and terror run?
For when her trouble came, and darkness pressed,
He smiled, and fought her madness with a pun.

Through all those years it was his task to keep
Her gentle heart serenely mystified.
If Fate's an artist, this should be his pride—
When, in that Christmas season, he lay dead,
She innocently looked. "I always said
That Charles is really handsome when asleep."

TO A GRANDMOTHER

At six o'clock in the evening,
The time for lullabies,
My son lay on my mother's lap
With sleepy, sleepy eyes!
(O drowsy little manny boy,
With sleepy, sleepy eyes!)

I heard her sing, and rock him,
And the creak of the swaying chair,
And the old dear cadence of the words
Came softly down the stair.

And all the years had vanished,
All folly, greed, and stain —
The old, old song, the creaking chair,
The dearest arms again!
(O lucky little manny boy,
To feel those arms again!)

DIARISTS

They catalogue their minutes: Now, now, now,
Is Actual, amid the fugitive;
Take ink and pen (they say) for that is how
We snare this flying life, and make it live.
So to their little pictures, and they sieve
Their happinesses: fields turned by the plough,
The afterglow that summer sunsets give,
The razor concave of a great ship's bow.

O gallant instinct, folly for men's mirth!
Type cannot burn and sparkle on the page.
No glittering ink can make this written word
Shine clear enough to speak the noble rage
And instancy of life. All sonnets blurred
The sudden mood of truth that gave them birth.

THE LAST SONNET

Suppose one knew that never more might one
Put pen to sonnet, well loved task; that now
These fourteen lines were all he could allow
To say his message, be forever done;
How he would scan the word, the line, the rhyme,
Intent to sum in dearly chosen phrase
The windy trees, the beauty of his days,
Life's pride and pathos in one verse sublime.
How bitter then would be regret and pang
For former rhymes he dallied to refine,
For every verse that was not crystalline....
And if belike this last one feebly rang,
Honor and pride would cast it to the floor
Facing the judge with what was done before.

THE SAVAGE

Civilization causes me
Alternate fits: disgust and glee.

Buried in piles of glass and stone
My private spirit moves alone,

Where every day from eight to six
I keep alive by hasty tricks.

But I am simple in my soul;
My mind is sullen to control.

At dusk I smell the scent of earth,
And I am dumb—too glad for mirth.

I know the savors night can give,
And then, and then, I live, I live!

No man is wholly pure and free,
For that is not his destiny,

But though I bend, I will not break:
And still be savage, for Truth's sake.

God damns the easily convinced
(Like Pilate, when his hands he rinsed).

ST. PAUL'S AND WOOLWORTH

I stood on the pavement
Where I could admire
Behind the brown chapel
The cream and gold spire.

Above, gilded Lightning
Swam high on his ball—
I saw the noon shadow
The church of St. Paul.

And was there a meaning?
(My fancy would run),
Saint Paul in the shadow,
Saint Frank in the sun!

ADVICE TO A CITY

O city, cage your poets! Hem them in
And roof them over from the April sky—
Clatter them round with babble, ceaseless din,
And drown their voices with your thunder cry.

Forbid their free feet on the windy hills,
And harness them to daily ruts of stone—
(In florists' windows lock the daffodils)
And never, never let them be alone!

For they are curst, said poets, curst and lewd,
And freedom gives their tongues uncanny wit,
And granted silence, thought and solitude
They (absit omen!) might make Song of it.

So cage them in, and stand about them thick,
And keep them busy with their daily bread;
And should their eyes seem strange, ah, then be quick
To interrupt them ere the word be said....

For, if their hearts burn with sufficient rage,
With wasted sunsets and frustrated youth,
Some day they'll cry, on some disturbing page,
The savage, sweet, unpalatable truth!

THE TELEPHONE DIRECTORY

No Malory of old romance,
No Crusoe tale, it seems to me,
Can equal in rich circumstance
This telephone directory.

No ballad of fair ladies' eyes,
No legend of proud knights and dames,
Can fill me with such bright surmise
As this great book of numbered names!

How many hearts and lives unknown,
Rare damsels pining for a squire,
Are waiting for the telephone
To ring, and call them to the wire.

Some wait to hear a loved voice say
The news they will rejoice to know
At Rome 2637 J
Or Marathon 1450!

And some, perhaps, are stung with fear
And answer with reluctant tread:
The message they expect to hear
Means life or death or daily bread.

A million hearts here wait our call,
All naked to our distant speech —
I wish that I could ring them all
And have some welcome news for each!

GREEN ESCAPE

At three o'clock in the afternoon
On a hot September day,
I began to dream of a highland stream
And a frostbit russet tree;
Of the swashing dip of a clipper ship
(White canvas wet with spray)
And the swirling green and milk-foam clean
Along her canted lee.

I heard the quick staccato click
Of the typist's pounding keys,
And I had to brood of a wind more rude
Than that by a motor fanned—
And I lay inert in a flannel shirt
To watch the rhyming seas
Deploy and fall in a silver sprawl
On a beach of sun-blanched sand.

There is no desk shall tame my lust
For hills and windy skies;
My secret hope of the sea's blue slope
No clerkly task shall dull;
And though I print no echoed hint
Of adventures I devise,
My eyes still pine for the comely line
Of an outbound vessel's hull.

When I elope with an autumn day

And make my green escape,
I'll leave my pen to tamer men
Who have more docile souls;
For forest aisles and office files
Have a very different shape,
And it's hard to woo the ocean blue
In a row of pigeon holes!

VESPER SONG FOR COMMUTERS

(Instead of "Marathon" the commuter may substitute the name of his favorite suburb)

The stars are kind to Marathon,
How low, how close, they lean!
They jostle one another
And do their best to please—
Indeed, they are so neighborly
That in the twilight green
One reaches out to pick them
Behind the poplar trees.

The stars are kind to Marathon,
And one particular
Bright planet (which is Vesper)
Most lucid and serene,
Is waiting by the railway bridge,
The Good Commuter's Star,
The Star of Wise Men coming home
On time, at 6:15!

THE ICE WAGON

I'd like to split the sky that roofs us down,
Break through the crystal lid of upper air,
And tap the cool still reservoirs of heaven.
I'd empty all those unseen lakes of freshness
Down some vast funnel, through our stifled streets.

I'd like to pump away the grit, the dust,
Raw dazzle of the sun on garbage piles,
The droning troops of flies, sharp bitter smells,
And gush that bright sweet flood of unused air
Down every alley where the children gasp.

And then I'd take a fleet of ice wagons—
Big yellow creaking carts, drawn by wet horses,—
And drive them rumbling through the blazing slums.
In every wagon would be blocks of coldness,
Pale, gleaming cubes of ice, all green and silver,
With inner veins and patterns, white and frosty;
Great lumps of chill would drip and steam and shimmer,
And spark like rainbows in their little fractures.

And where my wagons stood there would be puddles,
A wetness and a sparkle and a coolness.
My friends and I would chop and splinter open
The blocks of ice. Bare feet would soon come pattering,
And some would wrap it up in Sunday papers,
And some would stagger home with it in baskets,
And some would be too gay for aught but sucking,

Licking, crunching those fast melting pebbles,
Gulping as they slipped down unexpected—
Laughing to perceive that secret numbness
Amid their small hot persons!

At every stop would be at least one urchin
Would take a piece to cool the sweating horses
And hold it up against their silky noses—
And they would start, and then decide they liked it.

Down all the sun-cursed byways of the town
Our wagons would be trailed by grimy tots,
Their ragged shirts half off them with excitement!
Dabbling toes and fingers in our leakage,
A lucky few up sitting with the driver,
All clambering and stretching grey-pink palms.

And by the time the wagons were all empty
Our arms and shoulders would be lame with chopping,
Our backs and thighs pain-shot, our fingers frozen.
But how we would recall those eager faces,
Red thirsty tongues with ice-chips sliding on them,
The pinched white cheeks, and their pathetic gladness.
Then we would know that arms were made for aching—

I wish to God that I could go tomorrow!

AT A MOVIE THEATRE

How well he spoke who coined the phrase
The picture palace! Aye, in sooth
A palace, where men's weary days
Are crowned with kingliness of youth.

Strange palace! Crowded, airless, dim,
Where toes are trod and strained eyes smart,
We watch a wand of brightness limn
The old heroics of the heart.

Romance again hath us in thrall
And Love is sweet and always true,
And in the darkness of the hall
Hands clasp—as they were meant to do.

Remote from peevish joys and ills
Our souls, pro tem, are purged and free:
We see the sun on western hills,
The crumbling tumult of the sea.

We are the blond that maidens crave,
Well balanced at a dozen banks;
By sleight of hand we haste to save
A brown-eyed life, nor stay for thanks!

Alas, perhaps our instinct feels
Life is not all it might have been,
So we applaud fantastic reels
Of shadow, cast upon a screen!

SONNETS IN A LODGING HOUSE

I

Each morn she crackles upward, tread by tread,
All apprehensive of some hideous sight:
Perhaps the Fourth Floor Back, who reads in bed,
Forgot his gas and let it burn all night—
The Sweet Young Thing who has the middle room,
She much suspects: for once some ink was spilled,
And then the plumber, in an hour of gloom,
Found all the bathroom pipes with tea-leaves filled.

II

No League of Nations scheme can make her gay—
She knows the rank duplicity of man;
Some folks expect clean towels every day,
They'll get away with murder if they can!
She tacks a card (alas, few roomers mind it)
Please leave the tub as you would wish to find it!

III

Men lodgers are the best, the Mrs. said:
They don't use my gas jets to fry sardines,
They don't leave red-hot irons on the spread,

They're out all morning, when a body cleans.
A man ain't so secretive, never cares
What kind of private papers he leaves lay,
So I can get a line on his affairs
And dope out whether he is likely pay.
But women! Say, they surely get my bug!
They stop their keyholes up with chewing gum,
Spill grease, and hide the damage with the rug,
And fry marshmallows when their callers come.
They always are behindhand with their rents—
Take my advice and let your rooms to gents!

THE MAN WITH THE HOE (PRESS)

About these roaring cylinders
Where leaping words and paper mate,
A sudden glory moves and stirs—
An inky cataract in spate!

What voice for falsehood or for truth,
What hearts attentive to be stirred—
How dimly understood, in sooth,
The power of the printed word!

These flashing webs and cogs of steel
Have shaken empires, routed kings,
Yet never turn too fast to feel
The tragedies of humble things.

O words, be strict in honesty,
Be just and simple and serene;
O rhymes, sing true, or you will be
Unworthy of this great machine!

DO YOU EVER FEEL LIKE GOD?

Across the court there rises the back wall
Of the Magna Carta Apartments.
The other evening the people in the apartment opposite
Had forgotten to draw their curtains.
I could see them dining: the well-blanched cloth,
The silver and glass, the crystal water jug,
The meat and vegetables; and their clean pink hands
Outstretched in busy gesture.

It was pleasant to watch them, they were so human;
So gay, innocent, unconscious of scrutiny.
They were four: an elderly couple,
A young man, and a girl—with lovely shoulders
Mellow in the glow of the lamp.
They were sitting over coffee, and I could see their hands
talking.

At last the older two left the room.
The boy and girl looked at each other....
Like a flash, they leaned and kissed.

Good old human race that keeps on multiplying!
A little later I went down the street to the movies,
And there I saw all four, laughing and joking together.
And as I watched them I felt like God—
Benevolent, all-knowing, and tender.

RAPID TRANSIT

(To Stephen Vincent Benét)

Climbing is easy and swift on Parnassus!
Knocking my pipe out, I entered a bookshop;
There found a book of verse by a young poet.
Comrades at once, how I saw his mind glowing!
Saw in his soul its magnificent rioting—
Then I ran with him on hills that were windy,
Basked and laughed with him on sun-dazzled beaches,
Glutted myself on his green and blue twilights,
Watched him disposing his planets in patterns,
Tumbling his colors and toys all before him.
I questioned life with him, his pulses my pulses;
Doubted his doubts, too, and grieved for his anguishes.
Salted long kinship and knew him from boy-hood—
Pulled out my own sun and stars from my knapsack,
Trying my trinkets with those of his finding—
And as I left the bookshop
My pipe was still warm in my hand.

CAUGHT IN THE UNDERTOW

Colin, worshipping some frail,
By self-deprecation sways her:
Calls himself unworthy male,
Hardly even fit to praise her.

But this tactic insincere
In the upshot greatly grieves him
When he finds the lovely dear
Quite implicitly believes him.

TO HIS BROWN-EYED MISTRESS

Who Rallied Him for Praising Blue Eyes in His Verses

If sometimes, in a random phrase
(For variation in my ditty),
I chance blue eyes, or gray, to praise
And seem to intimate them pretty—

It is because I do not dare
With too unmixed reiteration
To sing the browner eyes and hair
That are my true intoxication.

Know, then, that I consider brown
For ladies' eyes, the only color;
And deem all other orbs in town
(Compared to yours), opaquer, duller.

I pray, perpend, my dearest dear;
While blue-eyed maids the praise were drinking,
How insubstantial was their cheer—
It was of yours that I was thinking!

PEACE

What is this Peace
That statesmen sign?
How I have sought
To make it mine.

Where groaning cities
Clang and glow
I hunted, hunted,
Peace to know.

And still I saw
Where I passed by
Discarded hearts, —
Heard children cry.

By willowed waters
Brimmed with rain
I thought to capture
Peace again.

I sat me down
My Peace to hoard,
But Beauty pricked me
With a sword.

For in the stillness
Something stirred,

And I was crippled
For a word.

There is no peace
A man can find;
The anguish sits
His heart behind.

The eyes he loves,
The perfect breast,
Too exquisite
To give him rest.

This is his curse
Since brain began.
His penalty
For being man.

May, 1919

SONG, IN DEPRECATION OF PULCHRITUDE

Beauty (so the poets say),
Thou art joy and solace great;
Long ago, and far away
Thou art safe to contemplate,

Beauty. But when now and here,
Visible and close to touch,
All too perilously near,
Thou tormentest us too much!

In a picture, in a song,
In a novel's conjured scenes,
Beauty, that's where you belong,
Where perspective intervenes.

But, my dear, in rosy fact
Your appeal I have to shirk —
You disturb me, and distract
My attention from my work!

MOUNTED POLICE

Watchful, grave, he sits astride his horse,
Draped with his rubber poncho, in the rain;
He speaks the pungent lingo of "The Force,"
And those who try to bluff him, try in vain.

Inured to every mood of fool and crank,
Shrewdly and sternly all the crowd he cons:
The rain drips down his horse's shining flank,
A figure nobly fit for sculptor's bronze.

O knight commander of our city stress,
Little you know how picturesque you are!
We hear you cry to drivers who transgress:
"Say, that's a helva place to park your car!"

TO HIS MISTRESS, DEPLORING THAT HE IS NOT
AN ELIZABETHAN GALAXY

Why did not Fate to me bequeath an Utterance Elizabethan?
It would have been delight to me
If natus ante 1603.

My stuff would not be soon forgotten
If I could write like Harry Wotton.

I wish that I could wield the pen
Like William Drummond of Hawthornden.

I would not fear the ticking clock
If I were Browne of Tavistock.

For blithe conceits I would not worry
If I were Raleigh, or the Earl of Surrey.

I wish (I hope I am not silly?)
That I could juggle words like Lyly.

I envy many a lyric champion,
I. e., viz., e. g., Thomas Campion.

I creak my rhymes up like a derrick,
I ne'er will be a Robin Herrick.

My wits are dull as an old Barlow—
I wish that I were Christopher Marlowe.

In short, I'd like to be Philip Sidney,
Or some one else of that same kidney.

For if I were, my lady's looks
And all my lyric special pleading
Would be in all the future books,
And called, at college, Required Reading.

THE INTRUDER

As I sat, to sift my dreaming
To the meet and needed word,
Came a merry Interruption
With insistence to be heard.

Smiling stood a maid beside me,
Half alluring and half shy;
Soft the white hint of her bosom—
Escapade was in her eye.

"I must not be so invaded,"
(In an anger then I cried)—
"Can't you see that I am busy?
Tempting creature, stay outside!

"Pearly rascal, I am writing:
I am now composing verse—
Fie on antic invitation:
Wanton, vanish—fly—disperse!

"Baggage, in my godlike moment
What have I to do with thee?"
And she laughed as she departed—
"I am Poetry," said she.

TIT FOR TAT

I often pass a gracious tree
Whose name I can't identify,
But still I bow, in courtesy
It waves a bough, in kind reply.

I do not know your name, O tree
(Are you a hemlock or a pine?)
But why should that embarrass me?
Quite probably you don't know mine.

SONG FOR A LITTLE HOUSE

I'm glad our house is a little house,
Not too tall nor too wide:
I'm glad the hovering butterflies
Feel free to come inside.

Our little house is a friendly house.
It is not shy or vain;
It gossips with the talking trees,
And makes friends with the rain.

And quick leaves cast a shimmer of green
Against our whited walls,
And in the phlox, the courteous bees
Are paying duty calls.

THE PLUMPUPPETS

When little heads weary have gone to their bed,
When all the good nights and the prayers have been said,
Of all the good fairies that send bairns to rest
The little Plumpuppets are those I love best.

If your pillow is lumpy, or hot, thin and flat,
The little Plumpuppets know just what they're at;
They plump up the pillow, all soft, cool and fat—
The little Plumpuppets plump-up it!

The little Plumpuppets are fairies of beds:
They have nothing to do but to watch sleepy heads;
They turn down the sheets and they tuck you in tight,
And they dance on your pillow to wish you good night!

No matter what troubles have bothered the day,
Though your doll broke her arm or the pup ran away;
Though your handies are black with the ink that was spilt—
Plumpuppets are waiting in blanket and quilt.

If your pillow is lumpy, or hot, thin and flat,
The little Plumpuppets know just what they're at;
They plump up the pillow, all soft, cool and fat—
The little Plumpuppets plump-up it!

DANDY DANDELION

When Dandy Dandelion wakes
And combs his yellow hair,
The ant his cup of dewdrop takes
And sets his bed to air;
The worm hides in a quilt of dirt
To keep the thrush away,
The beetle dons his pansy shirt—
They know that it is day!

And caterpillars haste to milk
The cowslips in the grass;
The spider, in his web of silk,
Looks out for flies that pass.
These humble people leap from bed,
They know the night is done:
When Dandy spreads his golden head
They think he is the sun!

Dear Dandy truly does not smell
As sweet as some bouquets;
No florist gathers him to sell,
He withers in a vase;
Yet in the grass he's emperor,
And lord of high renown;
And grateful little folk adore
His bright and shining crown.

THE HIGH CHAIR

Grimly the parent matches wit and will:
Now, Weesy, three more spoons! See Tom the cat,
He'd drink it. You want to be big and fat
Like Daddy, don't you? (Careful now, don't spill!)
Yes, Daddy'll dance, and blow smoke through his nose,
But you must finish first. Come, drink it up—
(Splash!) Oh, you must keep both hands on the cup.
All gone? Now for the prunes....
                                    And so it goes.

This is the battlefield that parents know,
Where one small splinter of old Adam's rib
Withstands an entire household offering spoons.
No use to gnash your teeth. For she will go
Radiant to bed, glossy from crown to bib
With milk and cereal and a surf of prunes.

LOVE AT FIRST SIGHT

Not long ago I fell in love,
But unreturned is my affection—
The girl that I'm enamored of
Pays little heed in my direction.

I thought I knew her fairly well:
In fact, I'd had my arm around her;
And so it's hard to have to tell
How unresponsive I have found her.

For, though she is not frankly rude,
Her manners quite the wrong way rub me:
It seems to me ingratitude
To let me love her—and then snub me!

Though I'm considerate and fond,
She shows no gladness when she spies me—
She gazes off somewhere beyond
And doesn't even recognize me.

Her eyes, so candid, calm and blue,
Seem asking if I can support her
In the style appropriate to
A lady like her father's daughter.

Well, if I can't then no one can—
And let me add that I intend to:

She'll never know another man
So fit for her to be a friend to.

Not love me, eh? She better had!
By Jove, I'll make her love me one day;
For, don't you see, I am her Dad,
And she'll be three weeks old on Sunday!

AUTUMN COLORS

The chestnut trees turned yellow,
The oak like sherry browned,
The fir, the stubborn fellow,
Stayed green the whole year round.

But O the bonny maple
How richly he does shine!
He glows against the sunset
Like ruddy old port wine.

THE LAST CRICKET

When the bulb of the moon with white fire fills
And dead leaves crackle under the feet,
When men roll kegs to the cider mills
And chestnuts roast on every street;

When the night sky glows like a hollow shell
Of lustered emerald and pearl,
The kilted cricket knows too well
His doom. His tiny bagpipes skirl.

Quavering under the polished stars
In stubble, thicket, and frosty copse
The cricket blows a few choked bars,
And puts away his pipe—and stops.

TO LOUISE

(A Christmas Baby, Now One Year Old.)

Undaunted by a world of grief
You came upon perplexing days,
And cynics doubt their disbelief
To see the sky-stains in your gaze.

Your sudden and inclusive smile
And your emphatic tears, admit
That you must find this life worth while,
So eagerly you clutch at it!

Your face of triumph says, brave mite,
That life is full of love and luck—
Of blankets to kick off at night,
And two soft rose-pink thumbs to suck.

O loveliest of pioneers
Upon this trail of long surprise,
May all the stages of the years
Show such enchantment in your eyes!

By parents' patient buttonings,
And endless safety pins, you'll grow
To ribbons, garters, hooks and things,
Up to the Ultimate Trousseau—

But never, in your dainty prime,

Will you be more adored by me
Than when you see, this Great First Time,
Lit candles on a Christmas Tree!

December, 1919.

CHRISTMAS EVE

Our hearts to-night are open wide,
The grudge, the grief, are laid aside:
The path and porch are swept of snow,
The doors unlatched; the hearthstones glow—
No visitor can be denied.

All tender human homes must hide
Some wistfulness beneath their pride:
Compassionate and humble grow
Our hearts to-night.

Let empty chair and cup abide!
Who knows? Some well-remembered stride
May come as once so long ago—
Then welcome, be it friend or foe!
There is no anger can divide
Our hearts to-night.

EPITAPH ON THE PROOFREADER OF THE
ENCYCLOPEDIA BRITANNICA

Majestic tomes, you are the tomb
Of Aristides Edward Bloom,
Who labored, from the world aloof,
In reading every page of proof.

From A to And, from Aus to Bis
Enthusiasm still was his;
From Cal to Cha, from Cha to Con
His soft-lead pencil still went on.

But reaching volume Fra to Gib,
He knew at length that he was sib
To Satan; and he sold his soul
To reach the section Pay to Pol.

Then Pol to Ree, and Shu to Sub
He staggered on, and sought a pub.
And just completing Vet to Zym,
The motor hearse came round for him.

He perished, obstinately brave:
They laid the Index on his grave.

THE MUSIC BOX

At six—long ere the wintry dawn—
There sounded through the silent hall
To where I lay, with blankets drawn
Above my ears, a plaintive call.

The Urchin, in the eagerness
Of three years old, could not refrain;
Awake, he straightway yearned to dress
And frolic with his clockwork train.

I heard him with a sullen shock.
His sister, by her usual plan,
Had piped us aft at 3 o'clock—
I vowed to quench the little man.

I leaned above him, somewhat stern,
And spoke, I fear, with emphasis—
Ah, how much better, parents learn,
To seal one's censure with a kiss!

Again the house was dark and still,
Again I lay in slumber's snare,
When down the hall I heard a trill,
A tiny, tinkling, tuneful air—

His music-box! His best-loved toy,
His crib companion every night;
And now he turned to it for joy
While waiting for the lagging light.

How clear, and how absurdly sad
Those tingling pricks of sound unrolled;
They chirped and quavered, as the lad
His lonely little heart consoled.

Columbia, the Ocean's Gem—
(Its only tune) shrilled sweet and faint.
He cranked the chimes, admiring them
In vigil gay, without complaint.

The treble music piped and stirred,
The leaping air that was his bliss;
And, as I most contritely heard,
I thanked the all-unconscious Swiss!

The needled jets of melody
Rang slowlier and died away—
The Urchin slept; and it was I
Who lay and waited for the day.

TO LUATH

(Robert Burns's Dog)

"Darling Jean" was Jean Armour, a "comely country lass" whom Burns met at a penny wedding at Mauchline. They chanced to be dancing in the same quadrille when the poet's dog sprang to his master and almost upset some of the dancers. Burns remarked that he wished he could get any of the lasses to like him as well as his dog did.

Some days afterward, Jean, seeing him pass as she was bleaching clothes on the village green, called to him and asked him if he had yet got any of the lasses to like him as well as his dog did.

That was the beginning of an acquaintance that coloured all of Burns's life.

—*Nathan Haskell Dole.*

Well, Luath, man, when you came prancing
All glee to see your Robin dancing,
His partner's muslin gown mischancing
You leaped for joy!
And little guessed what sweet romancing
You caused, my boy!

With happy bark, that moment jolly,
You frisked and frolicked, faithful collie;
His other dog, old melancholy,
Was put to flight—
But what a tale of grief and folly
You wagged that night!

Ah, Luath, tyke, your bonny master
Whose lyric pulse beat ever faster
Each time he saw a lass and passed her
His breast went bang!
In many a woful heart's disaster
He felt the pang!

Poor Robin's heart, forever burning,
Forever roving, ranting, yearning,
From you that heart might have been learning
To be less fickle!
Might have been spared so many a turning
And grievous prickle!

Your collie heart held but one notion —
When Robbie jigged in sprightly motion
You ran to show your own devotion
And gambolled too,
And so that tempest on love's ocean
Was due to you!

Well, it is ower late for preaching
And hearts are aye too hot for teaching!
When Robin with his eye beseeching
By greenside came,
Jeanie — poor lass — forgot her bleaching
And yours the blame!

THOUGHTS ON REACHING LAND

I had a friend whose path was pain—
Oppressed by all the cares of earth
Life gave him little chance to drain
His secret cisterns of rich mirth.

His work was hasty, harassed, vexed:
His dreams were laid aside, perforce,
Until—in this world, or the next....
(His trade? Newspaper man, of course!)

What funded wealth of tenderness,
What ingots of the heart and mind
He must uneasily repress
Beneath the rasping daily grind.

But now and then, and with my aid,
For fear his soul be wholly lost,
His devoir to the grape he paid
To call soul back, at any cost!

Then, liberate from discipline,
Undrugged by caution and control,
Through all his veins came flooding in
The virtued passion of his soul!

His spirit bared, and felt no shame:
With holy light his eyes would shine—

See Truth her acolyte reclaim
After the second glass of wine!

The self that life had trodden hard
Aspired, was generous and free:
The glowing heart that care had charred
Grew flame, as it was meant to be.

A pox upon the canting lot
Who call the glass the Devil's shape—
A greater pox where'er some sot
Defiles the honor of the grape.

Then look with reverence on wine
That kindles human brains uncouth—
There must be something part divine
In aught that brings us nearer Truth!

So—continently skull your fumes
(Here let our little sermon end)
And bless this X-ray that illumes
The secret bosom of your friend!

A SYMPOSIUM

There was a Russian novelist
Whose name was Solugubrious,
The reading circles took him up,
(They'd heard he was salubrious.)

The women's club of Cripple Creek
Soon held a kind of seminar
To learn just what his message was—
You know what bookworms women are.

The tea went round. After five cups
(You should have seen them bury tea)
Dear Mrs. Brown said what she liked
Was the great man's sincerity.

Sweet Mrs. Jones (how free she was
From all besetting vanity)
Declared that she loved even more
His broad and deep humanity.

Good Mrs. Smith, though she disclaimed
All thought of being critical,
Protested that she found his work
A wee bit analytical.

But Mrs. Black, the President,
Of wisdom found the pinnacle:

She said, "Dear me, I always think
Those Russians are so cynical."

Well, poor old Solugubrious,
It's true that they had heard of him;
But neither Brown, Jones, Smith, nor Black
Had ever read a word of him!

TO A TELEPHONE OPERATOR WHO HAS A BAD COLD

How hoarse and husky in my ear
Your usually cheerful chirrup:
You have an awful cold, my dear—
Try aspirin or bronchial syrup.

When I put in a call to-day
Compassion stirred my humane blood red
To hear you faintly, sadly, say
The number: Burray Hill dide hudred!

I felt (I say) quick sympathy
To hear you croak in the receiver—
Will you be sorry too for me
A month hence, when I have hay fever?

NURSERY RHYMES FOR THE TENDER-HEARTED

(Dedicated to Don Marquis.)

I

Scuttle, scuttle, little roach—
How you run when I approach:
Up above the pantry shelf.
Hastening to secrete yourself.

Most adventurous of vermin,
How I wish I could determine
How you spend your hours of ease,
Perhaps reclining on the cheese.

Cook has gone, and all is dark—
Then the kitchen is your park:
In the garbage heap that she leaves
Do you browse among the tea leaves?

How delightful to suspect
All the places you have trekked:
Does your long antenna whisk its
Gentle tip across the biscuits?

Do you linger, little soul,
Drowsing in our sugar bowl?
Or, abandonment most utter,
Shake a shimmy on the butter?

Do you chant your simple tunes
Swimming in the baby's prunes?
Then, when dawn comes, do you slink
Homeward to the kitchen sink?

Timid roach, why be so shy?
We are brothers, thou and I.
In the midnight, like yourself,
I explore the pantry shelf!

II

Rockabye, insect, lie low in thy den,
Father's a cockroach, mother's a hen.
And Betty, the maid, doesn't clean up the sink,
So you shall have plenty to eat and to drink.

Hushabye, insect, behind the mince pies:
If the cook sees you her anger will rise;
She'll scatter poison, as bitter as gall,
Death to poor cockroach, hen, baby and all.

III

There was a gay henroach, and what do you think,
She lived in a cranny behind the old sink—
Eggshells and grease were the chief of her diet;
She went for a stroll when the kitchen was quiet.

She walked in the pantry and sampled the bread,
But when she came back her old husband was dead:
Long had he lived, for his legs they were fast,
But the kitchen maid caught him and squashed him at last.

IV

I knew a black beetle, who lived down a drain,
And friendly he was though his manners were plain;
When I took a bath he would come up the pipe,
And together we'd wash and together we'd wipe.

Though mother would sometimes protest with a sneer
That my choice of a tub-mate was wanton and queer,
A nicer companion I never have seen:
He bathed every night, so he must have been clean.

Whenever he heard the tap splash in the tub
He'd dash up the drain-pipe and wait for a scrub,
And often, so fond of ablution was he,
I'd find him there floating and waiting for me.

But nurse has done something that seems a great shame:
She saw him there, waiting, prepared for a game:
She turned on the hot and she scalded him sore
And he'll never come bathing with me any more.

THE TWINS

C on was a thorn to brother Pro—
On Pro we often sicked him:
Whatever Pro would claim to know
Old Con would contradict him!

A PRINTER'S MADRIGAL

(Extremely technical)

I'd like to have you meet my wife!
I simply cannot keep from hinting
I've never seen, in all my life,
So fine a specimen of printing.

Her type is not some bold-face font,
Set solid. Nay! And I will say out
That no typographer could want
To see a better balanced layout.

A nice proportion of white space
There is for brown eyes to look large in,
And not a feature in her face
Comes anywhere too near the margin.

Locked up with all her sweet display
Her form will never pi. She's like a
Corrected proof marked stet, O. K. —
And yet she loves me, fatface **Pica!**

She has a fine one-column head,
And like a comma curves each eyebrow —
Her forehead has an extra lead
Which makes her seem a trifle highbrow.

Her nose, italicized brevier,
Too lovely to describe by penpoint;

Her mouth is set in pearl: her ear
And chin are comely Caslon ten-point.

Her cheeks (a pink parenthesis)
Make my pulse beat 14-em measure,
And such typography as this
Would make De Vinne scream with pleasure.

And so, of all typefounder chaps
Her father's best, in my opinion;
She is my nonpareil (in caps)
And I (in lower case) her minion.

I hope you will not stand aloof
Because my metaphors are shoppy;
Of her devotion I've a proof—
I tell the urchin, Follow Copy!

THE POET ON THE HEARTH

When fire is kindled on the dogs,
But still the stubborn oak delays,
Small embers laid above the logs
Will draw them into sudden blaze.

Just so the minor poet's part:
(A greater he need not desire)
The charcoals of his burning heart
May light some Master into fire!

O PRAISE ME NOT THE COUNTRY

O praise me not the country —
The meadows green and cool,
The solemn glow of sunsets, the hidden silver pool!
The city for my craving,
Her lordship and her slaving,
The hot stones of her paving
For me, a city fool!

O praise me not the leisure
Of gardened country seats,
The fountains on the terrace against the summer heats —
The city for my yearning,
My spending and my earning.
Her winding ways for learning,
Sing hey! the city streets!

O praise me not the country,
Her sycamores and bees,
I had my youthful plenty of sour apple trees!
The city for my wooing,
My dreaming and my doing;
Her beauty for pursuing,
Her deathless mysteries.

O praise me not the country,
Her evenings full of stars,
Her yachts upon the water with the wind among their
spars —

The city for my wonder,
Her glory and her blunder,
And O the haunting thunder
Of the Elevated cars!

A STONE IN ST. PAUL'S GRAVEYARD

(New York)

> *Here Lyes the Body of*
> *Iohn Jones the Son of*
> *Iohn Jones Who Departed*
> *This Life December the 13*
> *1768 Aged 4 Years & 4 Months & 2 Days*

Here, where enormous shadows creep,
He casts his childish shadow too:
How small he seems, beneath the steep
Great walls; his tender days, so few,
Lovingly numbered, every one—
John Jones, John Jones's little son.

O sunlight on the Lightning's wings!
Yet though our buildings skyward climb
Our heartbreaks are but little things
In the equality of Time.
The sum of life, for all men's stones:
He was John Jones, son of John Jones.

THE MADONNA OF THE CURB

On the curb of a city pavement,
By the ash and garbage cans,
In the stench and rolling thunder
Of motor trucks and vans,
There sits my little lady,
With brave but troubled eyes,
And in her arms a baby
That cries and cries and cries.

She cannot be more than seven;
But years go fast in the slums,
And hard on the pains of winter
The pitiless summer comes.
The wail of sickly children
She knows; she understands
The pangs of puny bodies,
The clutch of small hot hands.

In the deadly blaze of August,
That turns men faint and mad,
She quiets the peevish urchins

By telling a dream she had —
A heaven with marble counters,
And ice, and a singing fan;
And a God in white, so friendly,
Just like the drug-store man.
Her ragged dress is dearer

Than the perfect robe of a queen!
Poor little lass, who knows not
The blessing of being clean.
And when you are giving millions
To Belgian, Pole and Serb,
Remember my pitiful lady—
Madonna of the Curb!

THE ISLAND

A song for England?
Nay, what is a song for England?

Our hearts go by green-cliffed Kinsale
Among the gulls' white wings,
Or where, on Kentish forelands pale
The lighthouse beacon swings:
Our hearts go up the Mersey's tide,
Come in on Suffolk foam—
The blood that will not be denied
Moves fast, and calls us home!

Our hearts now walk a secret round
On many a Cotswold hill,
For we are mixed of island ground,
The island draws us still:
Our hearts may pace a windy turn
Where Sussex downs are high,
Or watch the lights of London burn,
A bonfire in the sky!

What is the virtue of that soil
That flings her strength so wide?
Her ancient courage, patient toil,
Her stubborn wordless pride?
A little land, yet loved therein
As any land may be,
Rejoicing in her discipline,
The salt stress of the sea.

Our hearts shall walk a Sherwood track,
Our lips taste English rain,
We thrill to see the Union Jack
Across some deep-sea lane;
Though all the world be of rich cost
And marvellous with worth,
Yet if that island ground were lost
How empty were the earth!

A song for England?
Lo, every word we speak's a song for England.

SUNDAY NIGHT

Two grave brown eyes, severely bent
Upon a memorandum book—
A sparkling face, on which are blent
A hopeful and a pensive look;
A pencil, purse, and book of checks
With stubs for varying amounts—
Elaine, the shrewdest of her sex,
Is busy balancing accounts.

Sedately, in the big armchair,
She, all engrossed, the audit scans—
Her pencil hovers here and there
The while she calculates and plans;
What's this? A faintly pensive frown
Upon her forehead gathers now—
Ah, does the butcher—heartless clown—
Beget that shadow on her brow?

A murrain on the tradesman churl
Who caused this fair accountant's gloom!
Just then—a baby's cry—my girl
Arose and swiftly left the room.
Then in her purse by stratagem
I thrust some bills of small amounts—
She'll think she had forgotten them,
And smile again at her accounts!

145

ENGLAND, JULY 1913

To Rupert Brooke

O England, England ... that July
How placidly the days went by!

Two years ago (how long it seems)
In that dear England of my dreams
I loved and smoked and laughed amain
And rode to Cambridge in the rain.
A careless godlike life was there!
To spin the roads with Shotover,
To dream while punting on the Cam,
To lie, and never give a damn
For anything but comradeship
And books to read and ale to sip,
And shandygaff at every inn
When The Gorilla rode to Lynn!
O world of wheel and pipe and oar
In those old days before the War.

O poignant echoes of that time!
I hear the Oxford towers chime,
The throbbing of those mellow bells
And all the sweet old English smells—

The Deben water, quick with salt,
The Woodbridge brew-house and the malt;
The Suffolk villages, serene
With lads at cricket on the green,

And Wytham strawberries, so ripe,
And Murray's Mixture in my pipe!

In those dear days, in those dear days,
All pleasant lay the country ways;
The echoes of our stalwart mirth
Went echoing wide around the earth
And in an endless bliss of sun
We lay and watched the river run.
And you by Cam and I by Isis
Were happy with our own devices.

Ah, can we ever know again
Such friends as were those chosen men,
Such men to drink, to bike, to smoke with,
To worship with, or lie and joke with?
Never again, my lads, we'll see
The life we led at twenty-three.
Never again, perhaps, shall I
Go flashing bravely down the High
To see, in that transcendent hour,
The sunset glow on Magdalen Tower.

Dear Rupert Brooke, your words recall
Those endless afternoons, and all
Your Cambridge—which I loved as one
Who was her grandson, not her son.
O ripples where the river slacks
In greening eddies round the "backs";
Where men have dreamed such gallant things
Under the old stone bridge at King's.
Or leaned to feed the silver swans
By the tennis meads at John's.
O Granta's water, cold and fresh,
Kissing the warm and eager flesh
Under the willow's breathing stir—

The bathing pool at Grantchester....
What words can tell, what words can praise
The burly savor of those days!

Dear singing lad, those days are dead
And gone for aye your golden head;
And many other well-loved men
Will never dine in Hall again.
I too have lived remembered hours
In Cambridge; heard the summer showers
Make music on old Heffer's pane
While I was reading Pepys or Taine.
Through Trumpington and Grantchester

I used to roll on Shotover;
At Hauxton Bridge my lamp would light
And sleep in Royston for the night.
Or to Five Miles from Anywhere
I used to scull; and sit and swear
While wasps attacked my bread and jam
Those summer evenings on the Cam.
(O crispy English cottage-loaves
Baked in ovens, not in stoves!
O white unsalted English butter
O satisfaction none can utter!)...

To think that while those joys I knew
In Cambridge, I did not know you.

July, 1915

CASUALTY

A well-sharp'd pencil leads one on to write:
When guns are cocked, the shot is guaranteed;
The primed occasion puts the deed in sight:
Who steals a book who knows not how to read?

Seeing a pulpit, who can silence keep?
A maid, who would not dream her ta'en to wife?
Men looking down from some sheer dizzy steep
Have (quite impromptu) leapt, and ended life.

A GRUB STREET RECESSIONAL

O noble gracious English tongue
Whose fibers we so sadly twist,
For caitiff measures he has sung
Have pardon on the journalist.

For mumbled meter, leaden pun,
For slipshod rhyme, and lazy word,
Have pity on this graceless one—
Thy mercy on Thy servant, Lord!

The metaphors and tropes depart,
Our little clippings fade and bleach:
There is no virtue and no art
Save in straightforward Saxon speech.

Yet not in ignorance or spite,
Nor with Thy noble past forgot
We sinned: indeed we had to write
To keep a fire beneath the pot.

Then grant that in the coming time,
With inky hand and polished sleeve,
In lucid prose or honest rhyme
Some worthy task we may achieve—

Some pinnacled and marbled phrase,
Some lyric, breaking like the sea,
That we may learn, not hoping praise,
The gift of Thy simplicity.

PRELIMINARY INSTRUCTIONS FOR A FUNERAL SERVICE: BEING A POEM IN FOUR STANZAS

Say this poor fool misfeatured all his days,
And could not mend his ways;
And say he trod
Most heavily upon the corns of God.

But also say that in his clabbered brain
There was the essential pain —
The idiot's vow
To tell his troubled Truth, no matter how.

Unhappy fool, you say, with pitiful air:
Who was he, then, and where?
Ah, you divine
He lives in your heart, as he lives in mine.